Dinosaur ? Questions

Written and illustrated by

Bernard Most

sandpiper

HOUGHTON MIFFLIN HARCOURT

Boston • New York

All rights reserved. Published in the United States by
Sandpiper, an imprint of Houghton Mifflin Harcourt
Publishing Company, Boston, Massachusetts. Originally
published in hardcover in the United States by Harcourt
Children's Books, an imprint of Houghton Mifflin Harcourt
Publishing Company, New York, 1995.

SANDPIPER and the SANDPIPER logo are trademarks
of Houghton Mifflin Harcourt Publishing Company.

www.sandpiperbooks.com

The text of this book is set in Chicken Soup.
The illustrations are in Pantone Tria markers
on Bainbridge board 172, hot-press finish.

The Library of Congress has cataloged
the hardcover edition as follows:
Most, Bernard.
Dinosaur questions/by Bernard Most.
1. Dinosaurs—Miscellanea—Juvenile literature.
[1. Dinosaurs.   2. Questions and answers.]   I. Title.
QE862.D5M6933   1995
567.9'1—dc20   94-42630
ISBN 978-0-15-292885-8
ISBN 978-0-15-206691-8 pb

Printed in Singapore
TWA 10 9 8 7 6 5 4 3 2 1

The author wishes to acknowledge the following sources
for the factual information contained within the text:
A Field Guide to Dinosaurs by David Lambert
Dinosaur Data by David Lambert
The New Illustrated Dinosaur Dictionary by
   Helen Roney Sattler
Dinosaur Encyclopedia by Don Lessem and Donald Glut
Dr. Phillip Currie of the University of Alberta

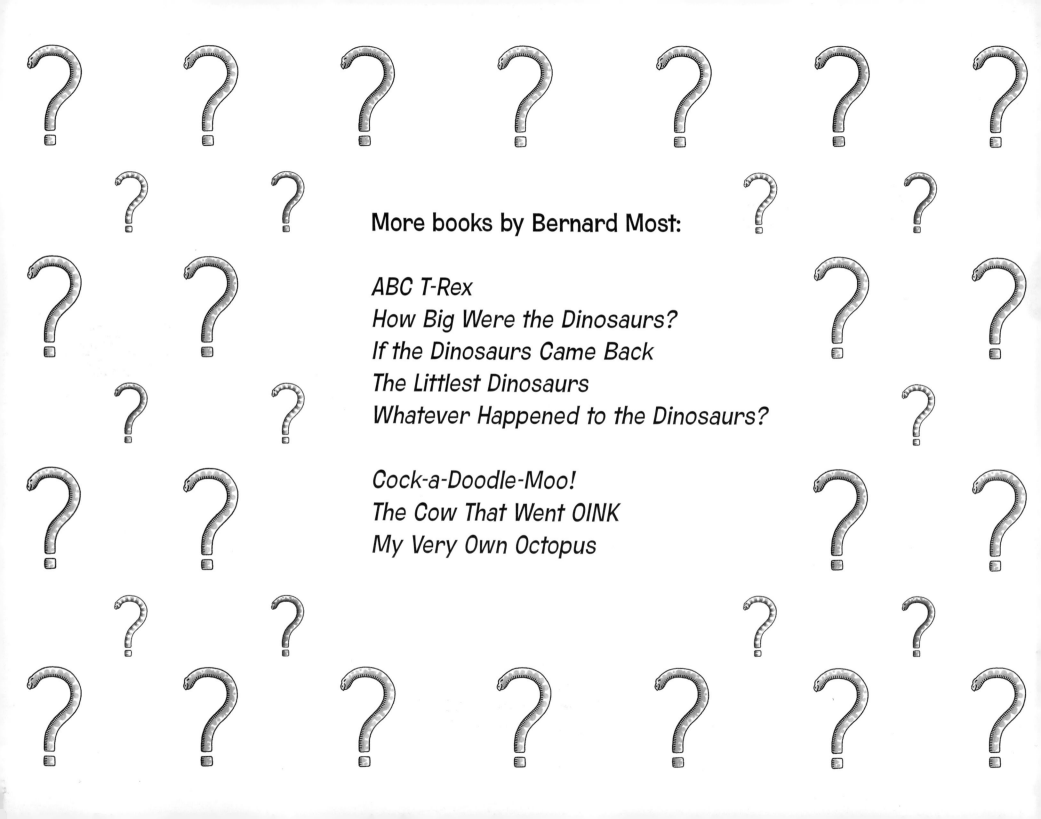

More books by Bernard Most:

ABC T-Rex
How Big Were the Dinosaurs?
If the Dinosaurs Came Back
The Littlest Dinosaurs
Whatever Happened to the Dinosaurs?

Cock-a-Doodle-Moo!
The Cow That Went OINK
My Very Own Octopus

To Diane D'Andrade
who wondered whether all the
dinosaur questions had been answered

Whenever I go to a museum to look at dinosaur fossils, or whenever I read a book at the library about dinosaurs, I think of so many dinosaur questions. There are so many things we don't know about dinosaurs. The more I learn about them and the more scientists change their theories about dinosaurs, the more dinosaur questions I have.

What colors were the dinosaurs?

Scientists used to think most dinosaurs were the same color as crocodiles. But they now think some dinosaurs may have had colorful spots, stripes, or patterns like many mammals, reptiles, fish, and tropical birds we see today. We'll probably never know what colors the dinosaurs really were. If you could color your own dinosaur, which colors would you choose?

We can guess what a dinosaur ate by studying its mouth and teeth. Sharp, serrated teeth were for tearing meat. Flatter, peglike, and spoon-shaped teeth were for collecting or crushing leaves and twigs. Horny, birdlike beaks were for cropping plants or cracking eggs. Sometimes food fossils are found alongside dinosaur fossils, giving us more clues about dinosaur dinners.

How much did dinosaurs weigh?

We don't know for sure! Scientists compare body weight, size, and posture of animals like elephants, hippos, and giraffes with dinosaur fossils and use the similarities to guess what dinosaurs might have weighed. Some "guesstimates": Stegosaurus weighed 2 tons, Triceratops weighed 5 tons, Apatosaurus weighed 30 tons, and Argentinosaurus may have weighed as much as 100 tons!

What did dinosaurs sound like?

We'll probably never know, but it's fun to guess! Dinosaur fossils show us that many dinosaurs could have had vocal structures and could have made sounds. The hollow tubes in the crests of some duck-billed dinosaurs suggest that they made loud, mooselike sounds. What do you think a dinosaur's voice might have sounded like?

How smart were dinosaurs?

Scientists have never found a dinosaur brain, but they can tell brain sizes from skull fossils. They have found that the biggest dinosaurs had the smallest brains. Stegosaurus, who weighed about 2 tons, had a tiny brain the size of a golf ball. Troodon (TROW-a-don), a member of a family of small, agile, two-legged dinosaurs with large brains, is believed to have been the smartest of them all.

Did any dinosaurs give birth to live babies?

Many dinosaur eggs, dinosaur nests, and even dinosaur hatchling fossils have been found. But there is no evidence that dinosaurs gave birth to live young, as mammals do. Since no Apatosaurus eggs have ever been found, some scientists wonder if that dinosaur might have given birth to live babies. Others think ostrichlike dinosaurs, because of their bone structure, might have also given birth to live young.

Most cold-blooded animals have lower body temperatures. They cannot control their body temperature, so to keep warm they move into the sun, and to cool down they move into the shade. To save energy, they move much more slowly than warm-blooded animals. Scientists used to think every dinosaur was cold-blooded. Now, many are changing their theories.

Warm-blooded animals have higher body temperatures. They have more energy and are more active than cold-blooded animals. Scientists think the large size of some dinosaurs and the plates and fins on other dinosaurs helped control body temperatures. They now think some dinosaurs may have been warm-blooded. Too bad nobody's ever taken a dinosaur's temperature!

The name of the well-known dinosaur Brontosaurus is a mistake. When Brontosaurus was discovered and named, scientists didn't realize it was the same dinosaur that had been discovered years earlier and named Apatosaurus. The correct scientific name is usually the first one given, but many people know this dinosaur by its second name. I still like to call it Brontosaurus!

How can scientists tell if fossils are male or female?

It's not easy to tell the difference! Scientists guess that dinosaurs found with eggs in their bodies were female. Based on knowledge of modern horned animals, scientists also guess that fossils with bigger facial bumps and horns, or fossils with showy crests, were male. But the truth is, we really don't know for sure which is which!

Which dinosaur ran the fastest?

Many dinosaurs were very, very speedy! Tracks of footprints help show us how fast some dinosaurs ran. The ostrichlike dinosaurs were among the fastest dinosaurs. If I had to bet on the speediest dinosaur ever, I would put all my money on Dromiceiomimus (droh-mee-see-a-MY-muss). Experts think it was able to run 40 miles per hour!

Did dinosaurs swim?

Scientists have argued for years over whether dinosaurs could swim. Fossilized footprints have been found that suggest a four-legged dinosaur's front feet touched the bottom of a lake while its body floated on the surface. Other tracks give clues that two-legged dinosaurs could swim, too. Dinosaurs spent a lot of time near water. Doesn't it make sense that many of them learned how to swim?

Why was one dinosaur named "good mother lizard"?

Among the most amazing dinosaur discoveries are giant nests containing many dinosaur babies of different ages. Scientists think these nests were like nurseries because the fossils show that adult dinosaurs brought food to their babies and cared for them. They named this dinosaur Maiasaura (my-a-SAW-ra) because it means "good mother lizard."

One of the biggest dinosaurs discovered so far is Seismosaurus (size-ma-SAW-russ). It was a four-legged plant eater found in New Mexico. Its bones seem to show that it was up to 170 feet long and weighed 80 to 100 tons. This giant dinosaur was almost twice as big and more than twice as heavy as Apatosaurus. That's a lot of dinosaur!

One of the littlest dinosaurs ever discovered is Mussaurus (moo-SAW-russ). Scientists found fossils of a baby Mussaurus near a nest in Argentina and nicknamed it "mouse lizard" because it was only 8 inches long. An adult Mussaurus would have been about 10 feet long. Do you think the biggest dinosaur would have enjoyed playing with the littlest dinosaur?

Which dinosaur had the longest neck?

The longest neck of any dinosaur (or for that matter, of any animal that ever lived) belonged to the four-legged plant eater Mamenchisaurus (ma-MEN-chee-saw-russ). Estimates of the length of its neck alone range from 35 to 49 feet. Just imagine how long it took for food to reach this dinosaur's stomach! I wonder if it was always hungry?

Did dinosaurs have ears?

Studies of fossil skulls suggest dinosaurs had internal ears like birds and crocodiles instead of external ears like rabbits and humans. Our knowledge of dinosaurs comes mostly from fossils of their "hard parts," or bones, rarely their "soft parts." We wouldn't know a rabbit had floppy ears if all we found were its bones. Isn't it possible some dinosaurs had ears like many living animals?

Why is Stegosaurus like a giant dinosaur puzzle?

Stegosaurus was the first dinosaur with plates to be discovered, and experts are still debating how to arrange the plates on Stegosaurus's back. Different arrangements have been tried: a single row of plates from neck to tail; pairs of plates in two rows; plates flopping outward on each side; and the version most experts agree on—two rows of overlapping plates.

Scientists are also still debating what the plates were used for. Were the plates used as armor for protection? Were they used as weapons? As fans for cooling? As solar panels to absorb heat? Were they used to make Stegosaurus appear bigger and more frightening? Or were they used to attract a mate? Isn't Stegosaurus like a giant dinosaur puzzle?

All we find of many dinosaurs is a single tooth or a few pieces of bone. How do we know dinosaurs didn't have whiskers? There are so many animals living today that have whiskers: cats, mice, rabbits, seals, and walruses. If walrus fossils were found hundreds of thousands of years from now, scientists might not be able to tell if it had whiskers!

Are birds dinosaur cousins?

This is one of the biggest dinosaur questions. Many dinosaurs had birdlike necks, birdlike claws, birdlike beaks, and birdlike bone structures. Some dinosaurs built nests and cared for their young. Some may have been warm-blooded like birds, and they may have even had feathers. Many scientists are convinced that birds are dinosaur cousins. What do you think?

How old did dinosaurs grow to be?

Growth rings in fossil bones suggest that some dinosaurs probably lived to a ripe old age. Scientists think that if dinosaurs were warm-blooded, they could have lived more than 120 years, and if cold-blooded, more than 200 years. But the guess is that most dinosaurs probably died of injury or disease long before they died of old age!

Where is the best place to dig for dinosaurs?

Dinosaur fossils have been found all over the world. They probably lived where you live, but I don't recommend digging up your backyard to search for fossils. Scientists are searching for dinosaur fossils right now, and they say the best places to look are deserts and areas where the soil has been worn away, exposing layers of ancient rock.

Why did dinosaurs disappear?

Did an asteroid hit the earth? Did clouds of dust block the sun, destroying the food chain? Did volcanoes cover the earth with volcanic ash, wiping out plant life? Did climate changes make life difficult for dinosaurs? Or did dinosaurs simply change into birds? Why didn't crocodiles, lizards, and insects disappear, too? Someday scientists may dig up clues to answer the biggest dinosaur question of all!

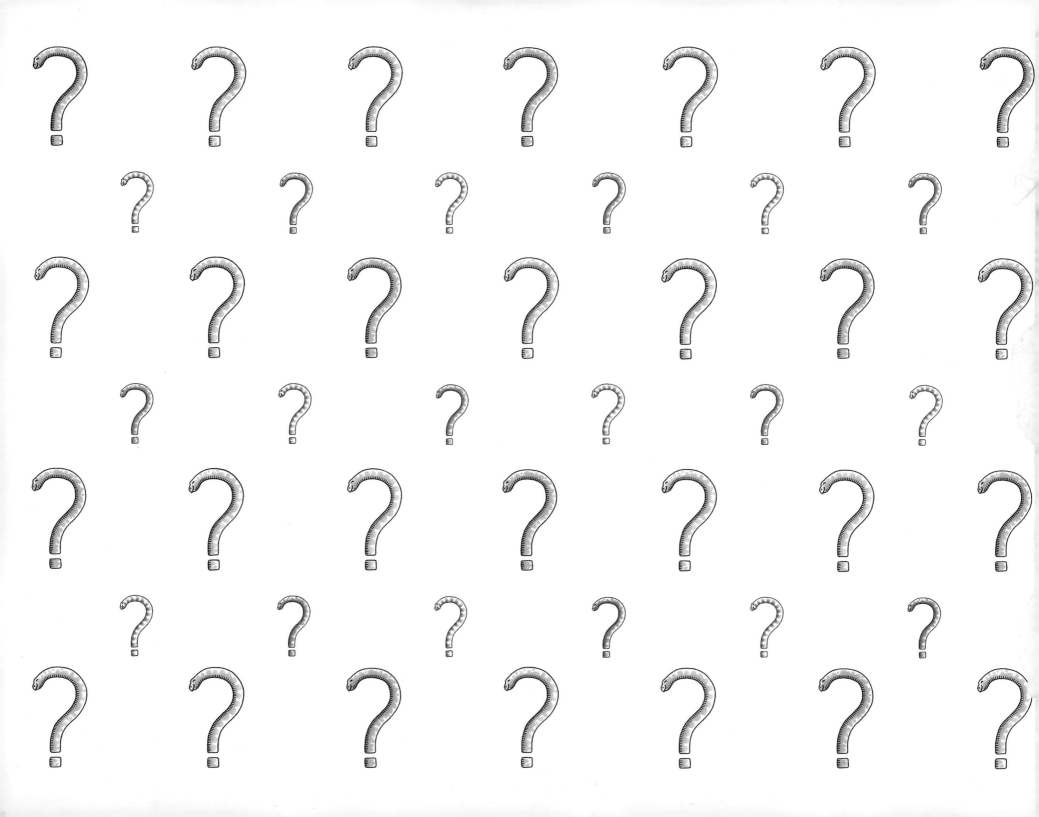